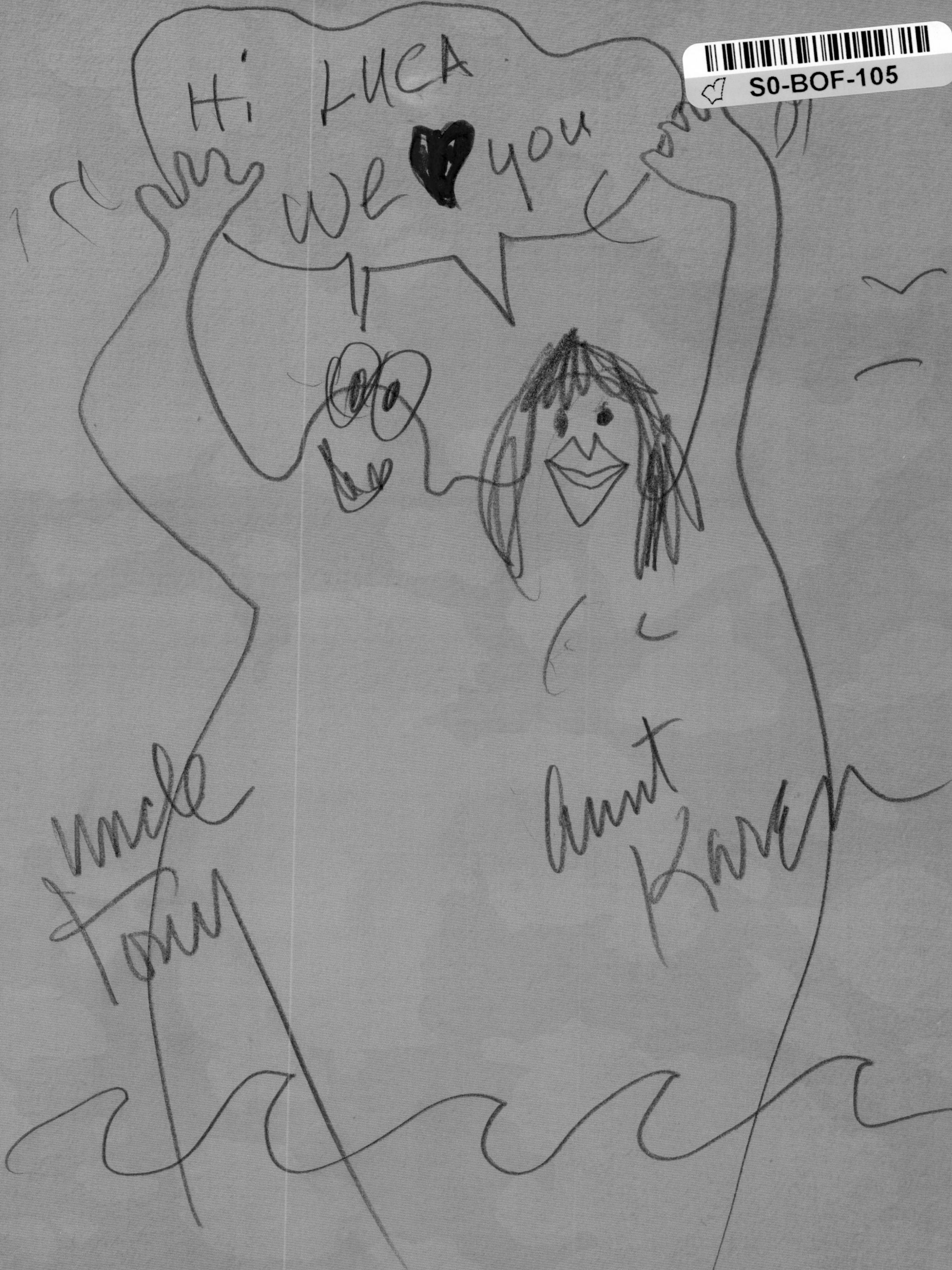
Hi LUCA
WE ♥ you
Uncle Tony
Aunt Karen

Thanks to all the staff and volunteers at
Coachella Valley Horse Rescue, who do such amazing
work saving horses and who introduced me to Guapo.

Thanks also to the stellar staff at Mascot Books for
believing in Guapo's story and for your professional
guidance in making this book come to life.

www.mascotbooks.com

Guapo's Giant Heart: The True Story of the Calf Who Kept Growing

For more information, please contact:
Mascot Books
620 Herndon Parkway, Suite 320
Herndon, VA 20170
info@mascotbooks.com

Library of Congress Control Number: 2021916702

CPSIA Code: PRT1021A
ISBN-13: 978-1-63755-093-9

Printed in the United States

GUAPO'S GIANT HEART

THE TRUE STORY OF THE CALF WHO KEPT GROWING

**JANET ZAPPALA
AND WENDY PERKINS**

Illustrated by Lara Calleja

ONE, TWO, THREE little calves lay huddled together in the hay. Lynn watched them. They did not play. They did not make a sound. Three skinny, sad babies—but there was only room for one in Lynn's tiny barn!

She closed her eyes to think. Suddenly, something wet grabbed her hand! Lynn's eyes flew open. The first thing she saw was a white heart on the calf's forehead. The next thing she saw was the rest of his head, from his floppy, fuzzy ears to his wide mouth that was sucking on Lynn's hand.

Lynn leaned over the rail. Her finger traced the heart-shaped spot on the calf's forehead. "Aren't you friendly," she cooed. "And so handsome!" The little calf lifted his head and snuffled Lynn's face.

"Well," said Lynn, "I guess I don't have to decide, because you've chosen me!" She named him **GUAPO ('WAH-PŌH')**, which means "handsome" in Spanish.

Little Guapo stretched his neck up and rested his head on Lynn's shoulder. As she walked to the trailer feeding him a bottle of milk, Guapo followed, slurping and swallowing.

BUMP, BUMP, RATTLE! The truck and trailer rolled down the road to Lynn's farm. Lynn led Guapo into a stall. He sniffed the air—strange smells. A loud noise made him tremble.

"It's alright, Guapo," said Lynn. "That's just Barney." In the next stall, a donkey lifted his head and opened his mouth. "**BAAAAR-NEEEY**," he brayed, taking a step closer.

Guapo backed away, nervous. Barney stood still and calm and softly puffed air toward the calf. Guapo moved forward and stretched his neck toward Barney.

The two said hello with a few gentle snorts and snuffles. Lynn watched, smiling. Suddenly, a push from behind made her stumble.

A little goat shoved past Lynn, ducked between the rails, and ran into Guapo's stall. "Oh, Bambi," Lynn said. "I should have known YOU would come to meet our new friend."

Guapo turned his head this way and that, watching Bambi bounce around the stall. She stood on her hind legs, then dropped to scurry under the calf.

She ran behind and butted his rump, nibbled his tail, then scampered to Guapo's face and licked his nose. The little black calf pawed the ground playfully, then sprinted alongside Bambi as she pranced away. Guapo felt safe and happy in his new home.

The calf's days were filled with bottles of milk, warm hugs from Lynn, and fun with his many friends. Guapo, Barney, and Bambi ran in the pasture for hours.

Then, the tired friends curled up close together and napped in the shade of a tree. The chickens would sit on the calf's broad back, clucking softly in the sun.

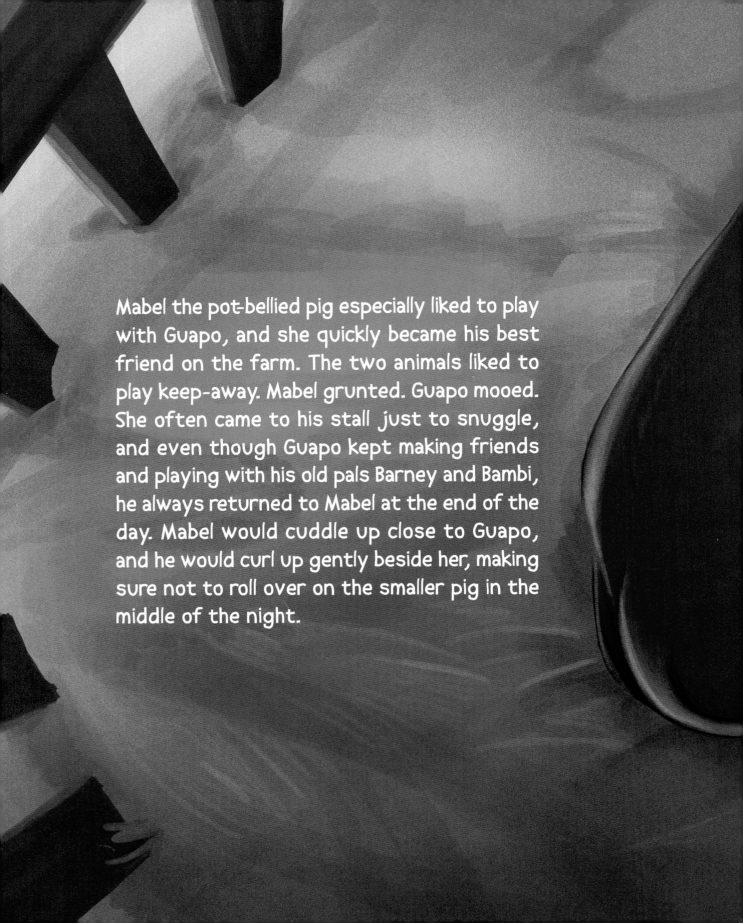

Mabel the pot-bellied pig especially liked to play with Guapo, and she quickly became his best friend on the farm. The two animals liked to play keep-away. Mabel grunted. Guapo mooed. She often came to his stall just to snuggle, and even though Guapo kept making friends and playing with his old pals Barney and Bambi, he always returned to Mabel at the end of the day. Mabel would cuddle up close to Guapo, and he would curl up gently beside her, making sure not to roll over on the smaller pig in the middle of the night.

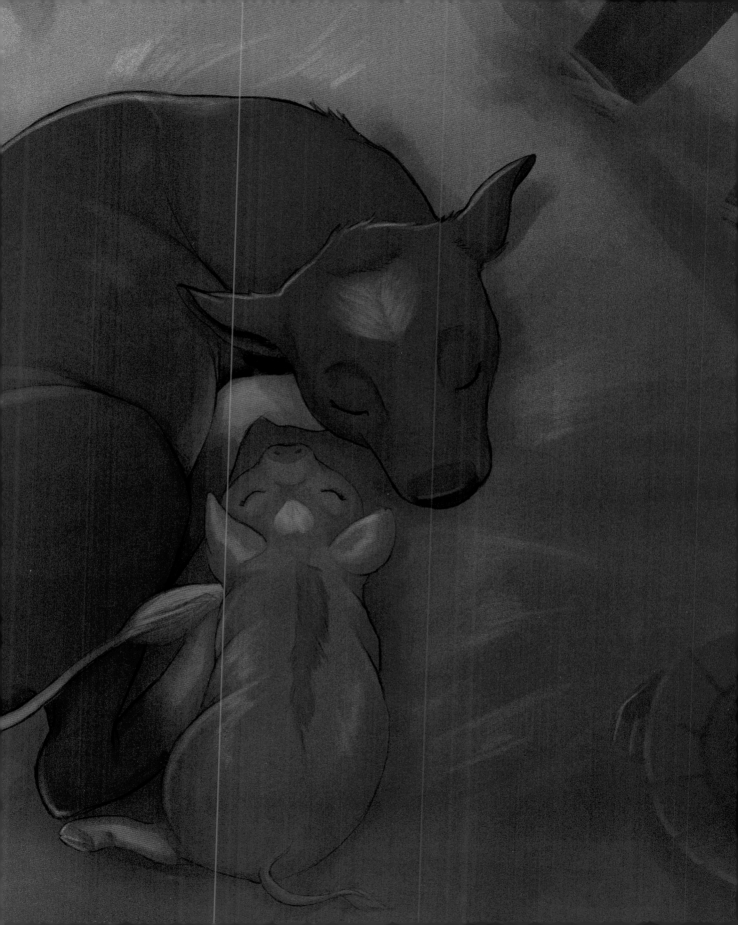

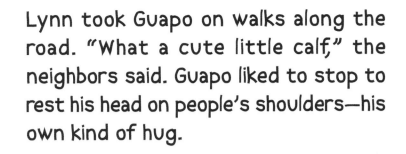

Lynn took Guapo on walks along the road. "What a cute little calf," the neighbors said. Guapo liked to stop to rest his head on people's shoulders—his own kind of hug.

With all the milk and fun with his friends, Guapo began to change. He wasn't a young calf anymore. His coat became shiny, and he started to grow into a large steer. Soon, he was eating hay.

"He's getting so big," people said. And Guapo just kept growing. "I think he's the biggest steer I've ever seen," one neighbor remarked.

But even with his massive and ever-growing size, Guapo's friends still saw him as the same little calf he had once been. They weren't afraid to run with him or play keep-away. The chickens still sat on his broad back in the midday sun.

Soon, Lynn saw that Guapo was getting too big for his stall. When he and Mabel curled up together each night, they would practically burst out of their stall. Eventually, Guapo got too big to cuddle up with Mabel, and even too big to sleep there himself. Guapo needed a larger space.

While Guapo played with his friends, Lynn looked on the computer and made phone calls.

One day, speaking softly, Lynn led Guapo into a big trailer. **BUMP, BUMP, RATTLE!** The truck and trailer rolled down the road for a long time.

When it stopped, giant Guapo sniffed the air—different smells. He looked around for his friends, but only Lynn was there. He hugged her with his huge head, and she stroked his neck for a long time before she left. Guapo felt lonely. He missed Lynn and his farm friends, especially Mabel.

But then, Guapo saw that he wasn't alone. Some goats, pigs, and cats stood a ways off and looked at him. "**HELLOOOOOOO**," Guapo mooed. The animals just stared. He playfully pawed the ground, but the animals ran away!

Each day, the animals came to look at the big steer. Guapo tried to make friends. He tilted his ears forward in a happy way. He stood still and calm.

He lay down to make himself smaller, but the other animals still stayed away. Guapo sighed and sadly closed his eyes.

Whenever Lynn came to visit, big Guapo gently stretched his head forward to hug her. But one day was different. He smelled something that made his heart happy. He watched as Lynn walked back to her trailer and opened the door. A snorting sound made his ears twitch. Guapo scrunched his nose and sniffed.

IT WAS MABEL!

Guapo lowered his head and his perky pot-bellied pig pal hurried over. The friends nuzzled noses. Guapo made his happy groaning sound. Mabel squealed with glee, her curly tail wagging happily. The two friends were reunited!

The other animals watched Mabel walk right up to Guapo. They saw him gently nibble Mabel's ear. They stared as Mabel snuggled with Guapo and made soft snuffling sounds. Each day they came to stare at the big steer and the little pig. Each day they came closer to Guapo and Mabel, until one day . . .

. . . THEY BEGAN TO PLAY, TOO! They rolled and ran, sunbathed and scratched, chased and chatted, butted and bucked.

CV HORSE RESCUE
COME BACK RANCH ANIMAL SANCTUARY

Guapo and Mabel had so many new friends! But the happiest time of day came at the end, when they nuzzled noses and cuddled—two forever friends, together in their new home.

ABOUT JANET ZAPPALA

Janet Zappala is an acclaimed journalist, six-time Emmy award-winning anchor and reporter, Golden Mike recipient, and an Associated Press First Place Award winner. She's worked as an anchor and host in several cities around the country, including Los Angeles, San Diego, Denver, and Philadelphia. Janet currently hosts *Good Food Matters*, a health and wellness cooking show streaming on various platforms, a project that combines her love of journalism with her experience as a certified nutritional consultant. She studied at the Global College of Natural Medicine in Northern California, and holds a second certification from the American Association of Drugless Practitioners. Janet's expert nutritional advice is gathered in the cookbook *My Italian Kitchen: Home-Style Recipes Made Lighter & Healthier,* released April 2010 and inspired by her mother and best friend, Mary, a spectacular cook in her own right. Above all these awards and accolades, though, Janet's proudest achievement is her beautiful grown son, who is a successful attorney and avid fisherman.

One of Janet's great passions is caring for animals, especially rescues. She volunteers and serves on the Advisory Council of the Coachella Valley Horse Rescue in Indio, California, where she met Guapo. Janet knew that the life lessons in his story would be valuable for parents and their children to share together. This is her first children's book.

ABOUT WENDY PERKINS

Wendy Perkins adores stories—reading, watching, listening to, and conjuring them. Animals, plants, and nature are her favorite things to write about, and children are her most-beloved audience. Wendy has written more than two dozen nonfiction children's books, created science and nature-themed curriculum, crafted content for kids' websites, and more. As a staff writer for the San Diego Zoo Wildlife Alliance, she shared stories that sparked understanding and appreciation of wildlife, and she hopes Guapo's story will do the same.

Wendy began her writing career by researching and writing exhibit labels and educational signs for zoos and aquariums. When she's not at her keyboard, you'll find her in her San Diego garden, where she grows vegetables, fruit, herbs, and a bounty of flowers that provide shelter and sustenance for urban wildlife.

MEET THE REAL ANIMALS WHO INSPIRED *GUAPO'S GIANT HEART*!

Bambi

Barney

Guapo and Barney

Lynn and Guapo

Photos courtesy of Lynn Jamerson.

Janet and Mabel

Janet and Guapo

Guapo

Let's Save A Horse Today!

CV HORSE RESCUE
COME BACK RANCH ANIMAL SANCTUARY
COACHELLA VALLEY MOUNTED RANGERS
INDIO, CA · EAGAR, AZ

GET INVOLVED

To learn how you can help rescued
animals in need at the Coachella Valley
Horse Rescue in Indio, California, and
Come Back Ranch Animal Sanctuary in
Eagar, Arizona, please visit

www.cvhorserescue.org.